Welcome to a Tale of Asgard...

Thor, the prince of Asgard, is a brash and impetuous youth. Never one to consider who he is or what he has, Thor's mind is always on who he will one day be and what the future holds for him. He feels he lives in the shadow of his father, Odin, ruler of all Asgard, and he hopes he can escape from Odin's shadow through noble deeds and valiant acts.

In order to please his father and hopefully prove his worth, Thor has agreed to undertake a quest on Odin's behalf: he and his two friends, Balder and Sif, must travel Asgard in search of four mystic elements which Odin hopes to forge into an enchanted sword. However, this impulsive decision does not sit well with Balder or Sif, as Thor has accepted the mission without consulting them first.

Their first task is to obtain a scale from the hide of the dragon Hakurei! Thor, along with the reluctant Balder and Sif, travels to Nastrond in hopes of quietly sneaking into Hakurei's lair to obtain a shed piece of the dragon's hide without incident. However, much to their surprise, they find the huge white dragon laying in wait for them. After a vicious battle, the teen trio was able to ultimately defeat Hakurei and escape unharmed with one of his scales, but not without further damaging the group's already fragile morale.

The disgruntled youths then traveled north to the snowy mountains of Niflheim for their second task, where they were to pluck a feather from the wing of the snow eagle Gnori. On the path up to Gnori's mountain aerie, the three were attacked by ice pixies. Thor, Balder and Sif stood their ground on the frozen trail and emerged victorious thanks to Sif's keen eye and strategic thinking. Gnori descended from his perch to check on the young Asgardians and congratulate them on their victory. Despite Thor's accusations, they discover that the ice pixies were not of Gnori's making. They obtain the snow eagle's feather and complete their task, but are now burdened with suspicions that evil forces may be trying to stand in the way of completing their quest!

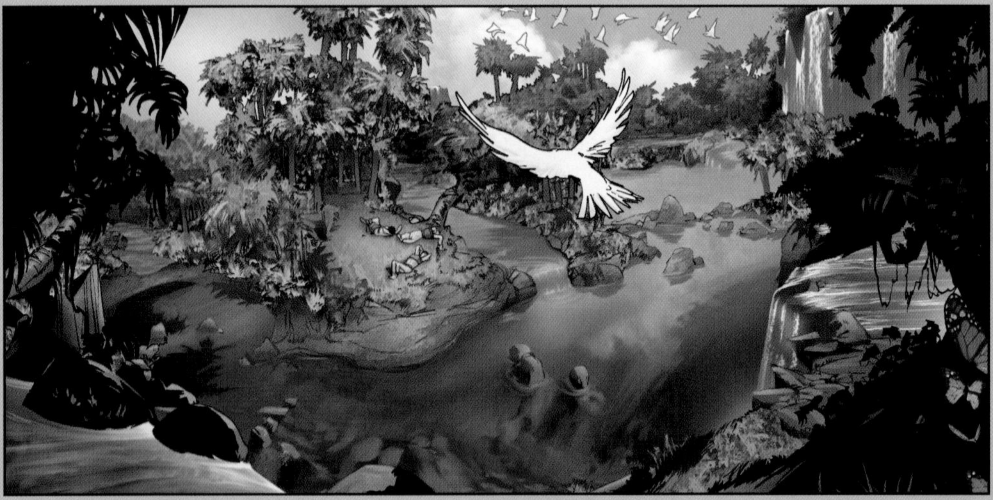

Part Four

The Jaws of Jennia

Akira Yoshida
WRITER

Greg Tocchini
PENCILER

Jay Leisten
INKER

Guru eFX
COLORIST

VC's Randy Gentile
LETTERER

Adi Granov
COVER ARTIST

MacKenzie Cadenhead
EDITOR

Ralph Macchio & C.B. Cebulski
CONSULTING EDITORS

Joe Quesada
EDITOR IN CHIEF

Dan Buckley
PUBLISHER

MARVEL

Spotlight

VISIT US AT
www.abdopublishing.com

Reinforced library bound edition published in 2007 by Spotlight, a division of the ABDO Publishing Group, Edina, Minnesota. Spotlight produces high quality reinforced library bound editions for schools and libraries. Published by agreement with Marvel Characters, Inc.

Library of Congress Cataloging-in-Publication Data

Yoshida, Akira.
Thor, son of Asgard / [Akira Yoshida, writer ; Greg Tocchini, penciler ; Jay Leisten, inker ; Guru e FX, colorist ; Adi Granov, cover artist ; Randy Gentile, letterer].
p. cm.
Cover title.
"Marvel Age."
Revisions of issues 1-6 of the serial Thor, son of Asgard.
Contents: pt. 1. The warriors teen -- pt. 2. The heat of Hakurei -- pt. 3. The nest of Gnori -- pt. 4. The jaws of Jennia -- pt. 5. The lake of Lilitha -- pt. 6. The trio triumphant.
ISBN-13: 978-1-59961-286-7 (pt. 1)
ISBN-10: 1-59961-286-0 (pt. 1)
ISBN-13: 978-1-59961-287-4 (pt. 2)
ISBN-10: 1-59961-287-9 (pt. 2)
ISBN-13: 978-1-59961-288-1 (pt. 3)
ISBN-10: 1-59961-288-7 (pt. 3)
ISBN-13: 978-1-59961-289-8 (pt. 4)
ISBN-10: 1-59961-289-5 (pt. 4)
ISBN-13: 978-1-59961-290-4 (pt. 5)
ISBN-10: 1-59961-290-9 (pt. 5)
ISBN-13: 978-1-59961-291-1 (pt. 6)
ISBN-10: 1-59961-291-7 (pt. 6)
1. Comic books, strips, etc. I. Tocchini, Greg. II. Title. III. Title: Warriors teen. IV. Title: Heat of Hakurei. V. Title: Nest of Gnori. VI. Title: Jaws of Jennia. VII. Title: Lake of Lilitha. VIII. Title: Trio triumphant.

PN6728.T64Y68 2007
791.5'73--dc22

2006050635

Spotlight

All Spotlight books are reinforced library binding and manufactured in the United States of America.

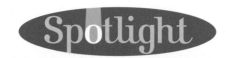

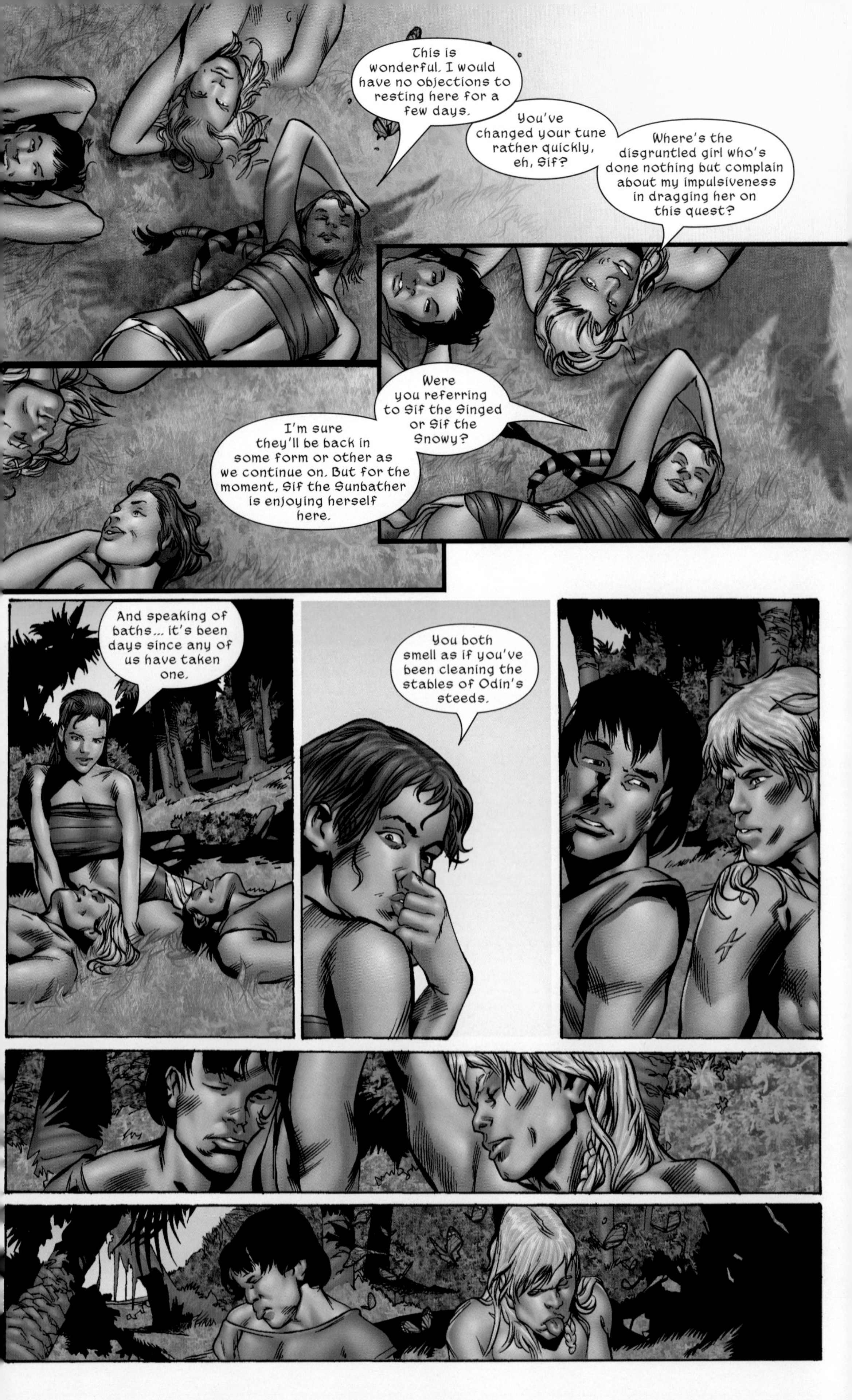
This is wonderful. I would have no objections to resting here for a few days.
You've changed your tune rather quickly, eh, Sif?
Where's the disgruntled girl who's done nothing but complain about my impulsiveness in dragging her on this quest?
Were you referring to Sif the Singed or Sif the Snowy?
I'm sure they'll be back in some form or other as we continue on. But for the moment, Sif the Sunbather is enjoying herself here.
And speaking of baths... it's been days since any of us have taken one.
You both smell as if you've been cleaning the stables of Odin's steeds.

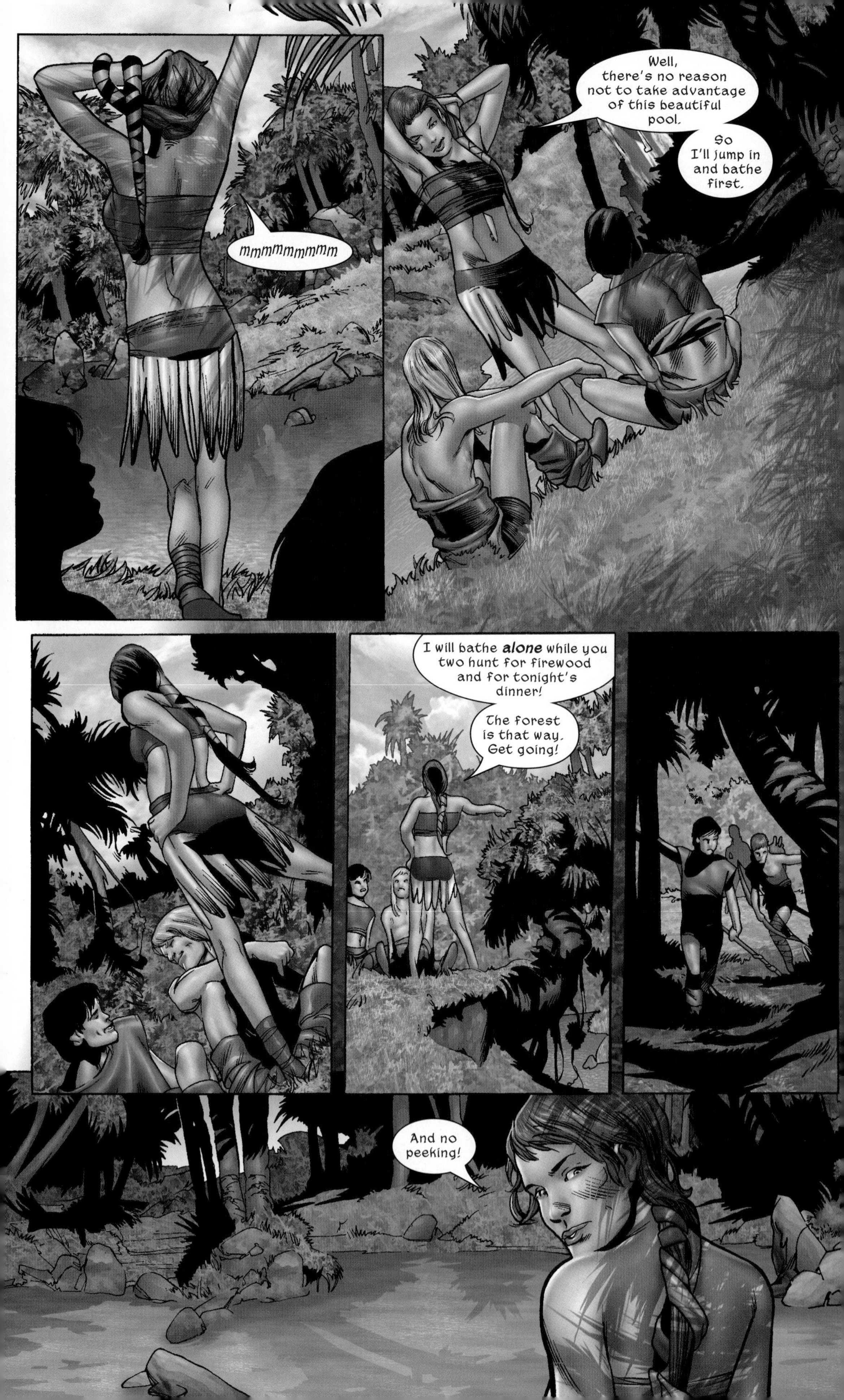
mmmmmmmmm
Well, there's no reason not to take advantage of this beautiful pool.
So I'll jump in and bathe first.
I will bathe alone while you two hunt for firewood and for tonight's dinner!
The forest is that way. Get going!
And no peeking!

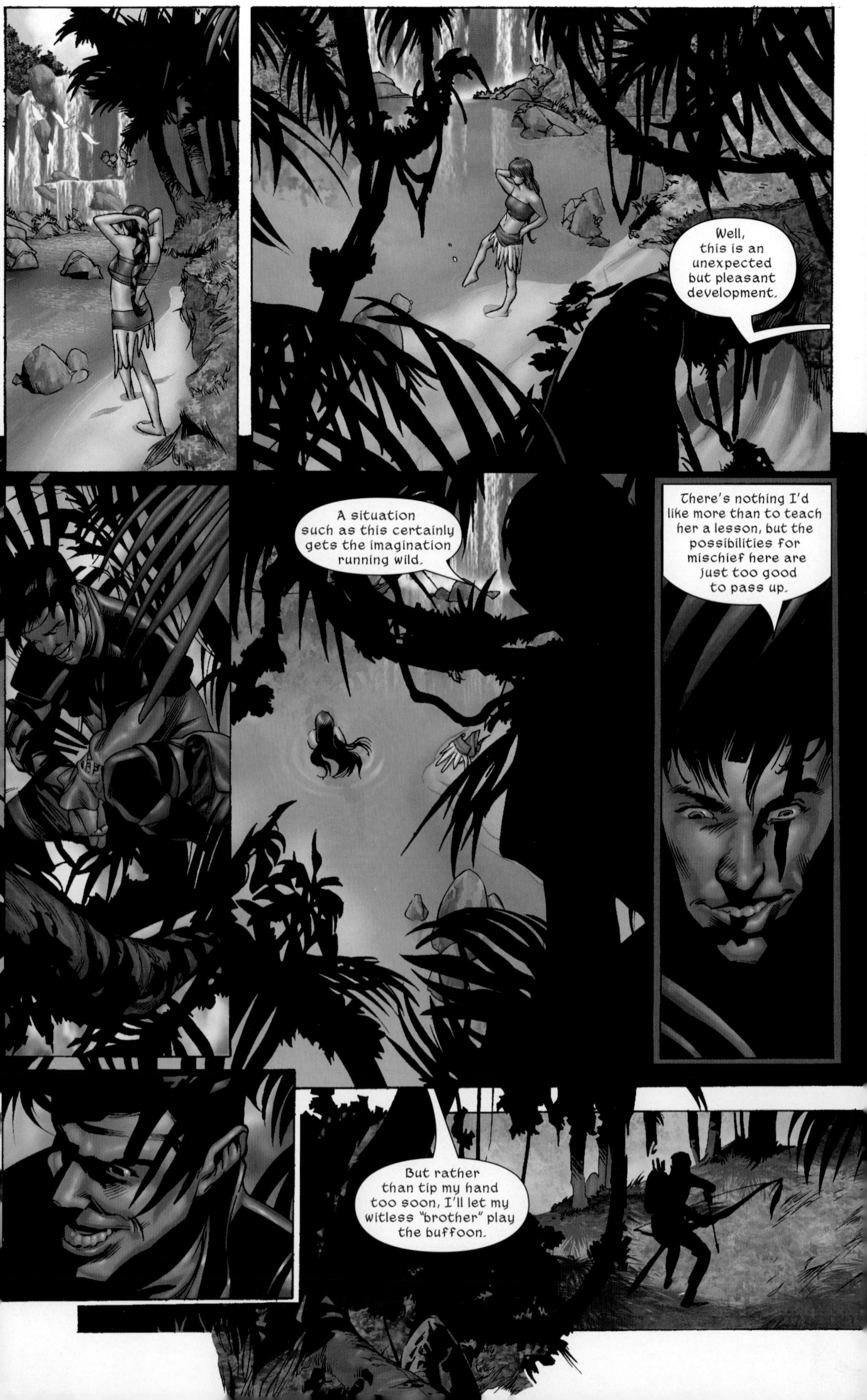
Well, this is an unexpected but pleasant development.
A situation such as this certainly gets the imagination running wild.
There's nothing I'd like more than to teach her a lesson, but the possibilities for mischief here are just too good to pass up.
But rather than tip my hand too soon, I'll let my witless "brother" play the buffoon.

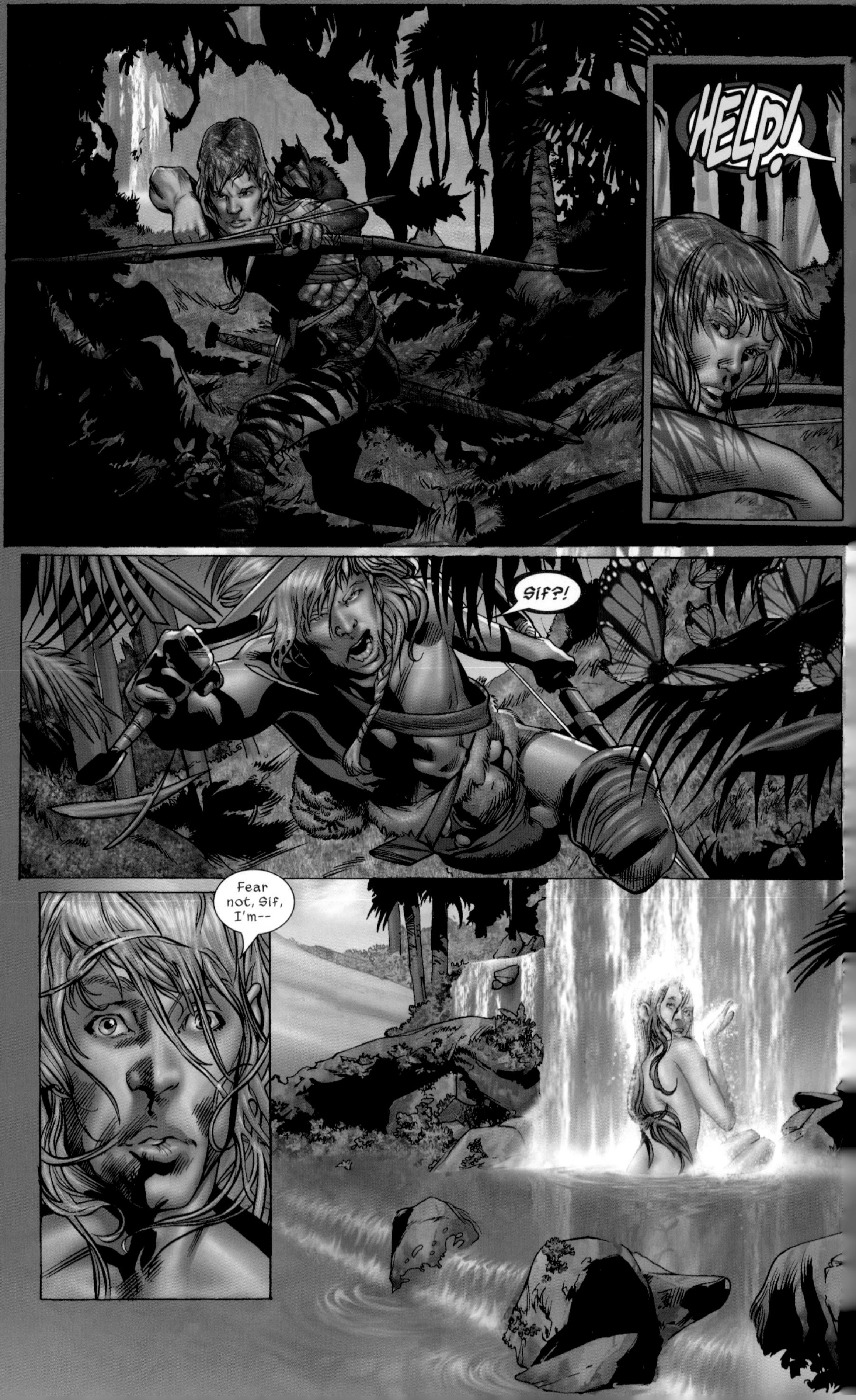
HELP!
Sif?!
Fear not, Sif, I'm--

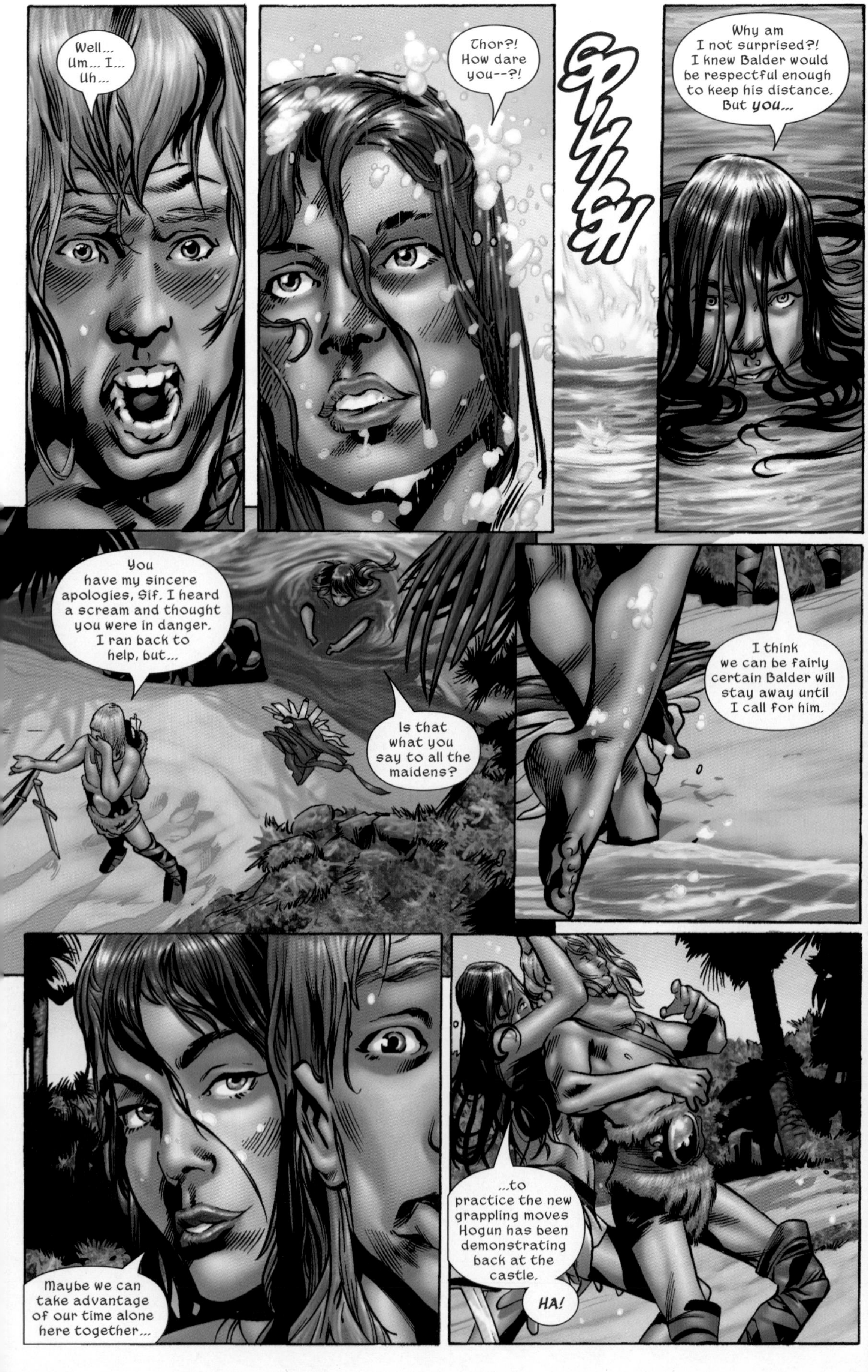
Well... Um... I... Uh...
Thor?! How dare you--?!
SPLLLSH
Why am I not surprised?! I knew Balder would be respectful enough to keep his distance. But *you*...
You have my sincere apologies, Sif. I heard a scream and thought you were in danger. I ran back to help, but...
Is that what you say to all the maidens?
I think we can be fairly certain Balder will stay away until I call for him.
Maybe we can take advantage of our time alone here together...
...to practice the new grappling moves Hogun has been demonstrating back at the castle.
HA!

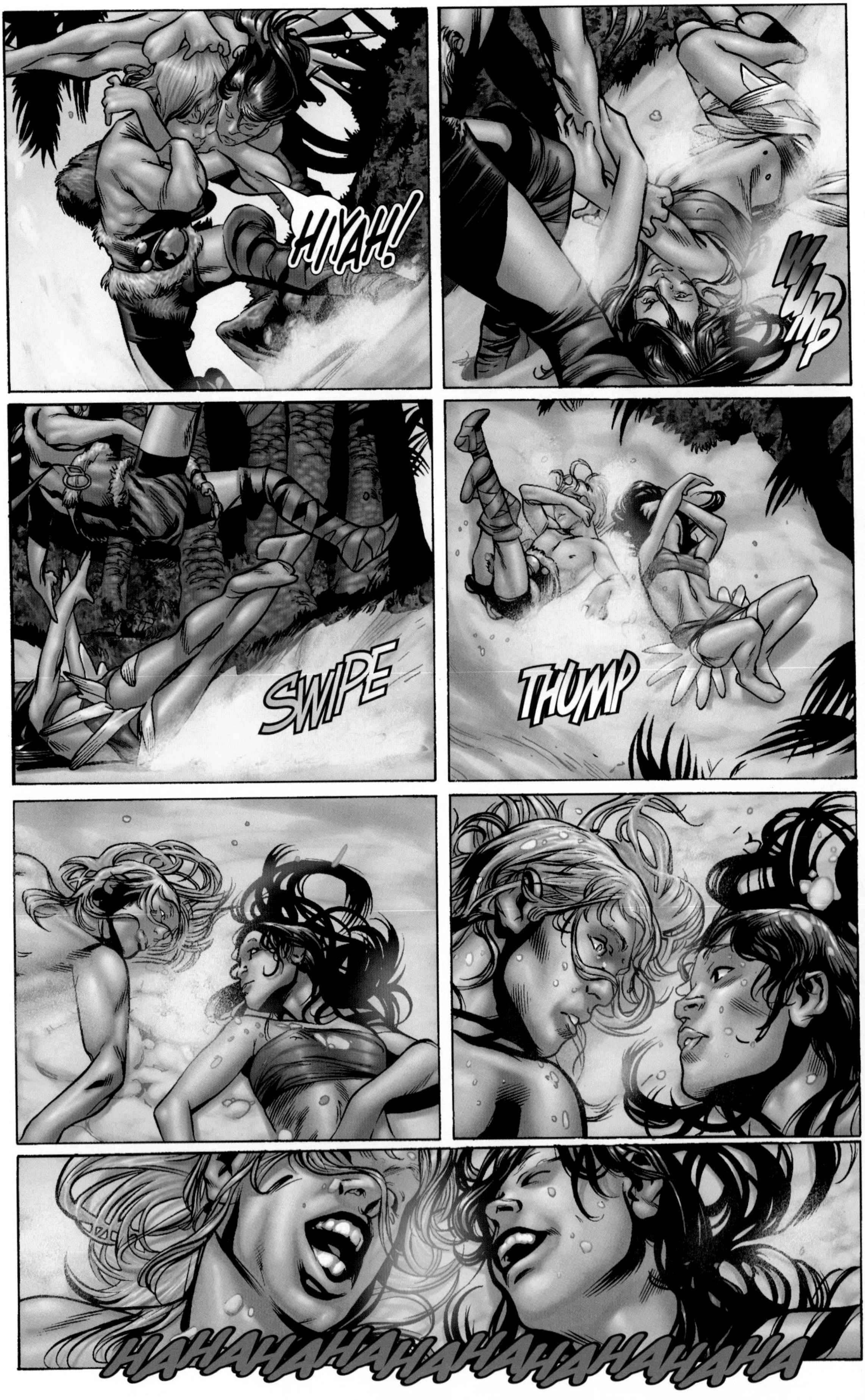
HIYAH!
WUMP
SWIPE
THUMP
HAHAHAHAHAHAHAHAHAHAHAHA

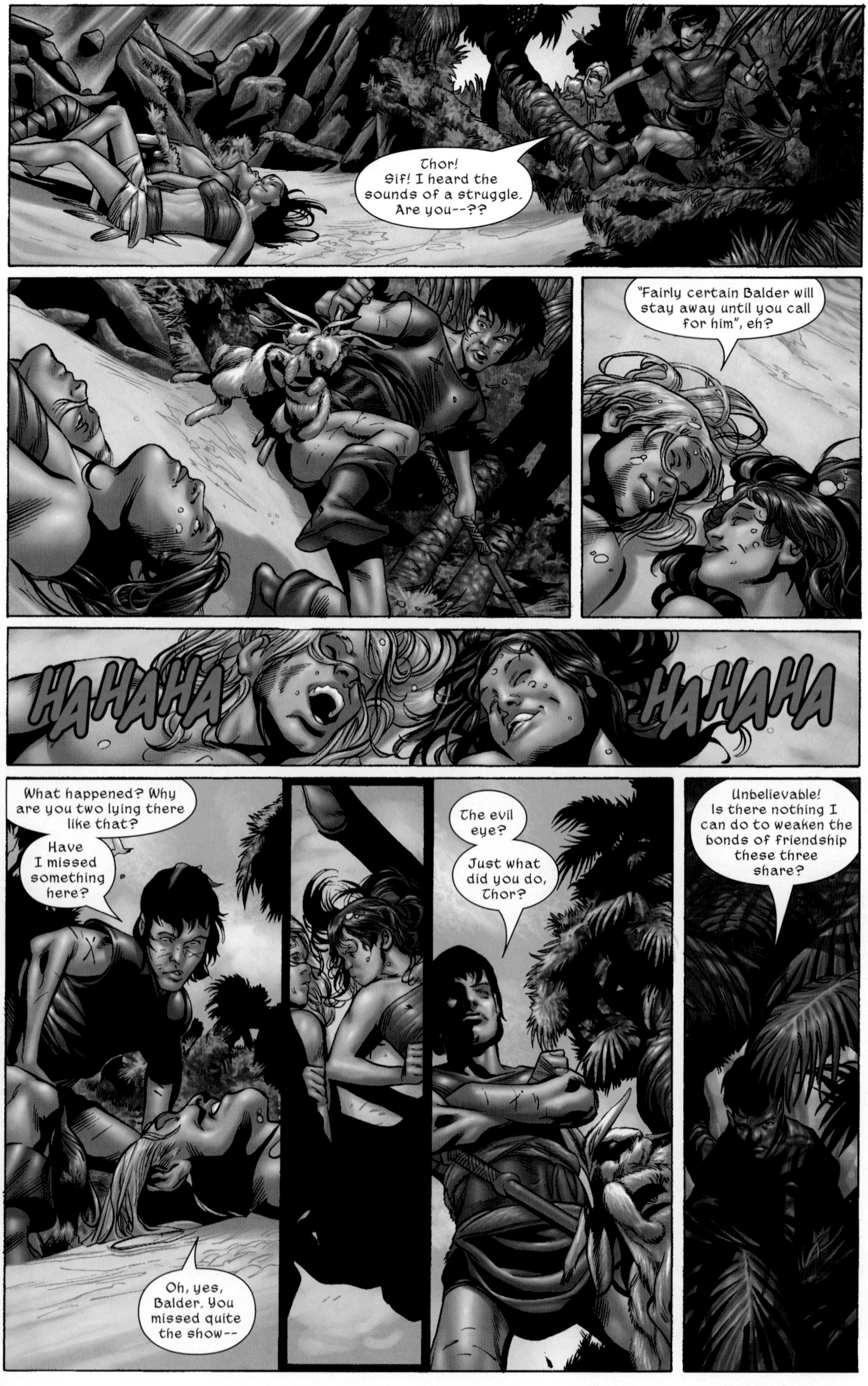
Thor!
Sif! I heard the sounds of a struggle.
Are you--??
"Fairly certain Balder will stay away until you call for him", eh?
HAHAHA
HAHAHA
What happened? Why are you two lying there like that?
Have I missed something here?
Oh, yes, Balder. You missed quite the show--
The evil eye?
Just what did you do, Thor?
Unbelievable!
Is there nothing I can do to weaken the bonds of friendship these three share?

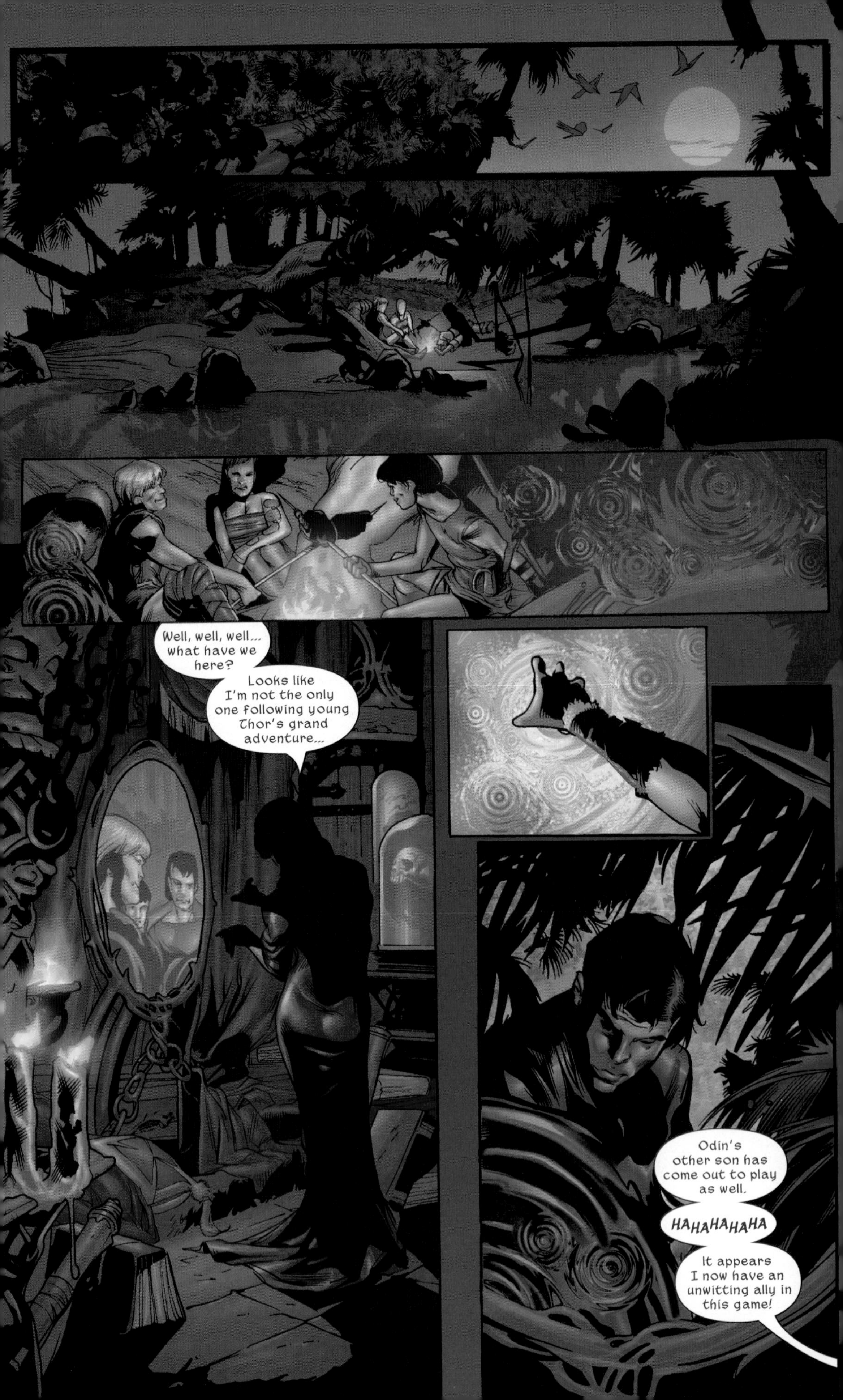
Well, well, well... what have we here?
Looks like I'm not the only one following young Thor's grand adventure...
Odin's other son has come out to play as well.
HAHAHAHAHA
It appears I now have an unwitting ally in this game!

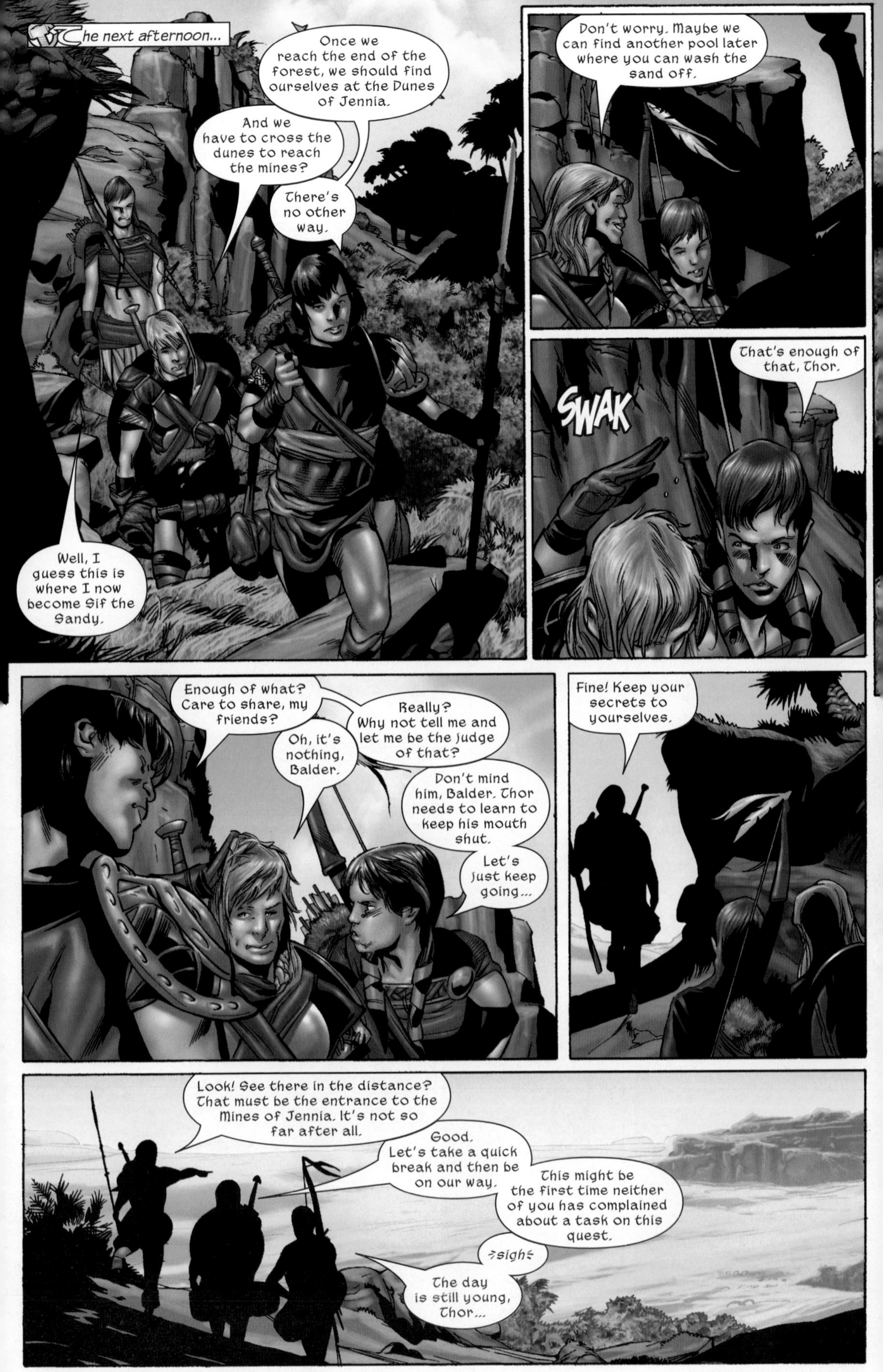
The next afternoon...
Once we reach the end of the forest, we should find ourselves at the Dunes of Jennia.
And we have to cross the dunes to reach the mines?
There's no other way.
Well, I guess this is where I now become Sif the Sandy.
Don't worry. Maybe we can find another pool later where you can wash the sand off.
SWAK
That's enough of that, Thor.
Enough of what? Care to share, my friends?
Oh, it's nothing, Balder.
Really? Why not tell me and let me be the judge of that?
Don't mind him, Balder. Thor needs to learn to keep his mouth shut.
Let's just keep going...
Fine! Keep your secrets to yourselves.
Look! See there in the distance? That must be the entrance to the Mines of Jennia. It's not so far after all.
Good. Let's take a quick break and then be on our way.
This might be the first time neither of you has complained about a task on this quest.
sigh
The day is still young, Thor...

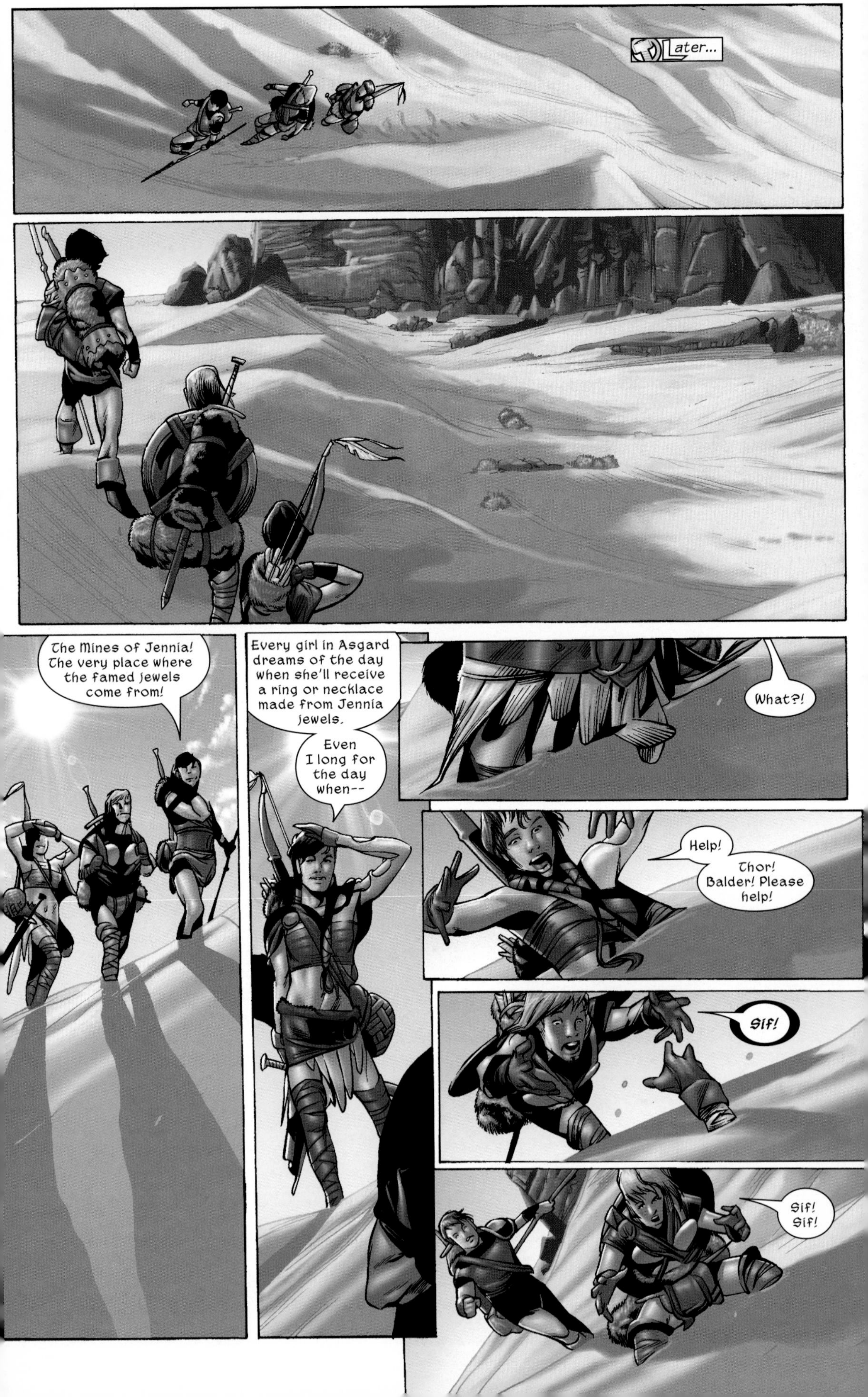
Later...
The Mines of Jennia! The very place where the famed jewels come from!
Every girl in Asgard dreams of the day when she'll receive a ring or necklace made from Jennia jewels.
Even I long for the day when--
What?!
Help!
Thor! Balder! Please help!
Sif!
Sif! Sif!

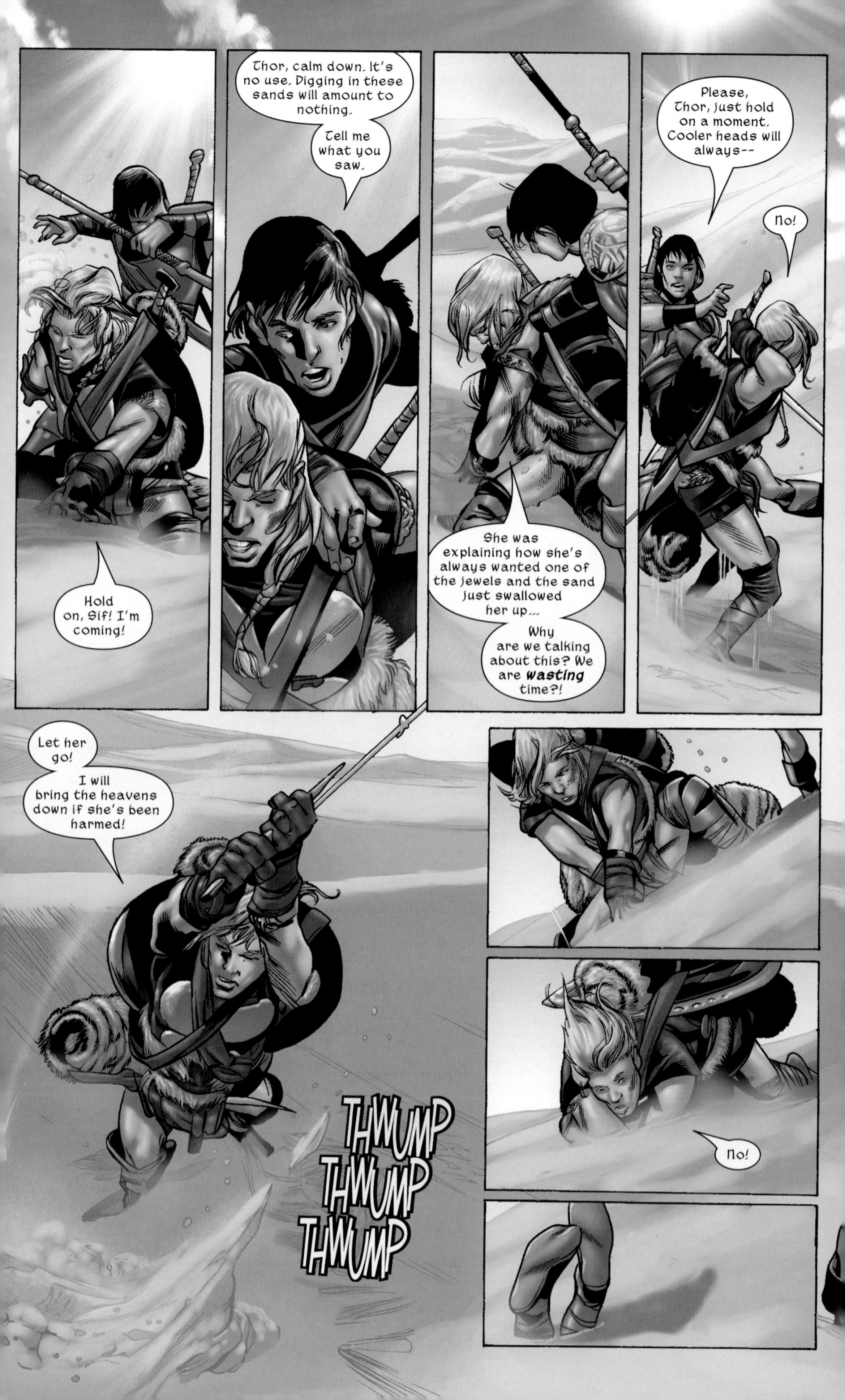
Hold on, Sif! I'm coming!
Thor, calm down. It's no use. Digging in these sands will amount to nothing.
Tell me what you saw.
She was explaining how she's always wanted one of the jewels and the sand just swallowed her up...
Why are we talking about this? We are *wasting* time?!
Please, Thor, just hold on a moment. Cooler heads will always--
No!
Let her go!
I will bring the heavens down if she's been harmed!
THWUMP THWUMP THWUMP
No!

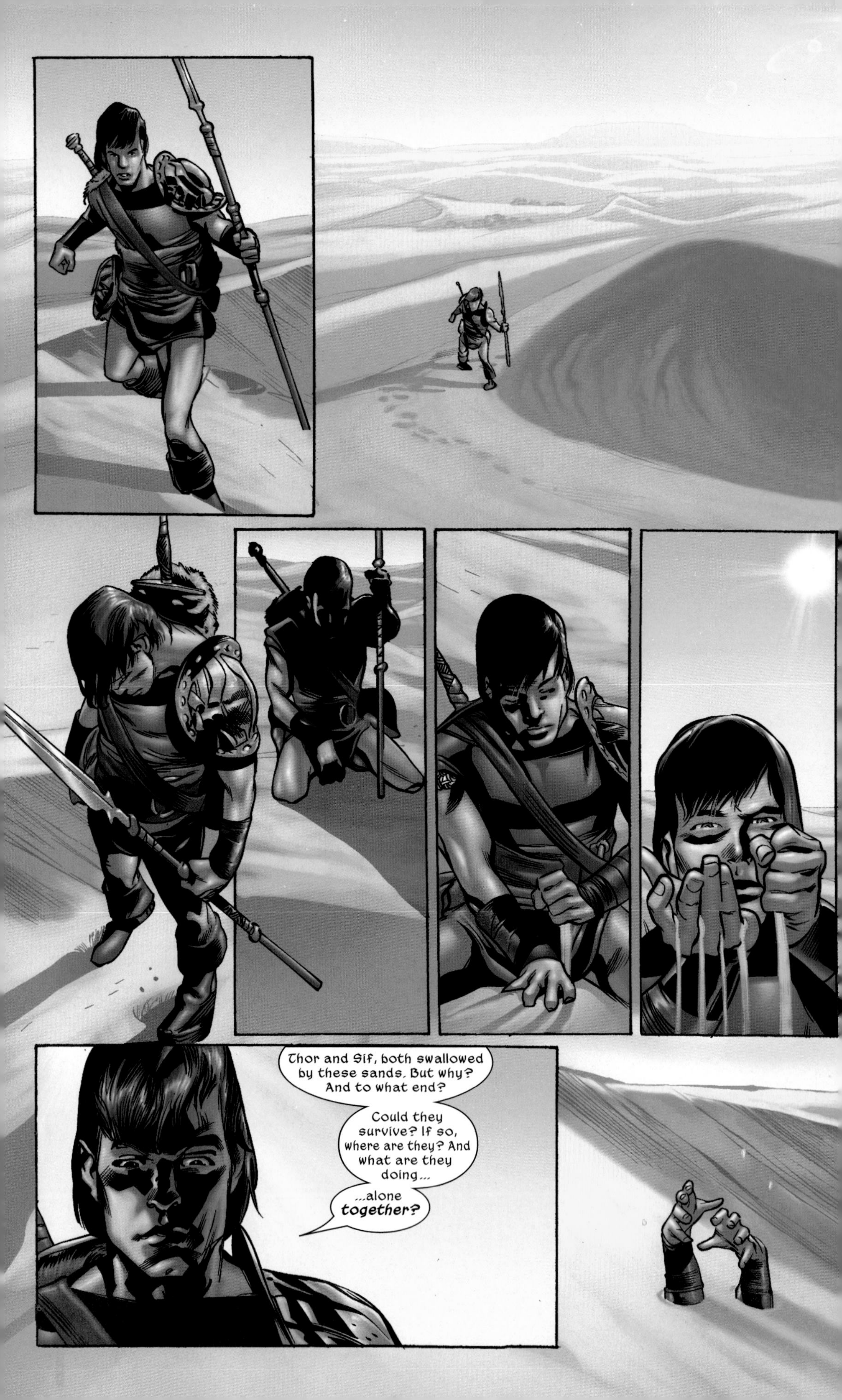

Thor and Sif, both swallowed by these sands. But why? And to what end?
Could they survive? If so, where are they? And what are they doing...
...alone *together?*

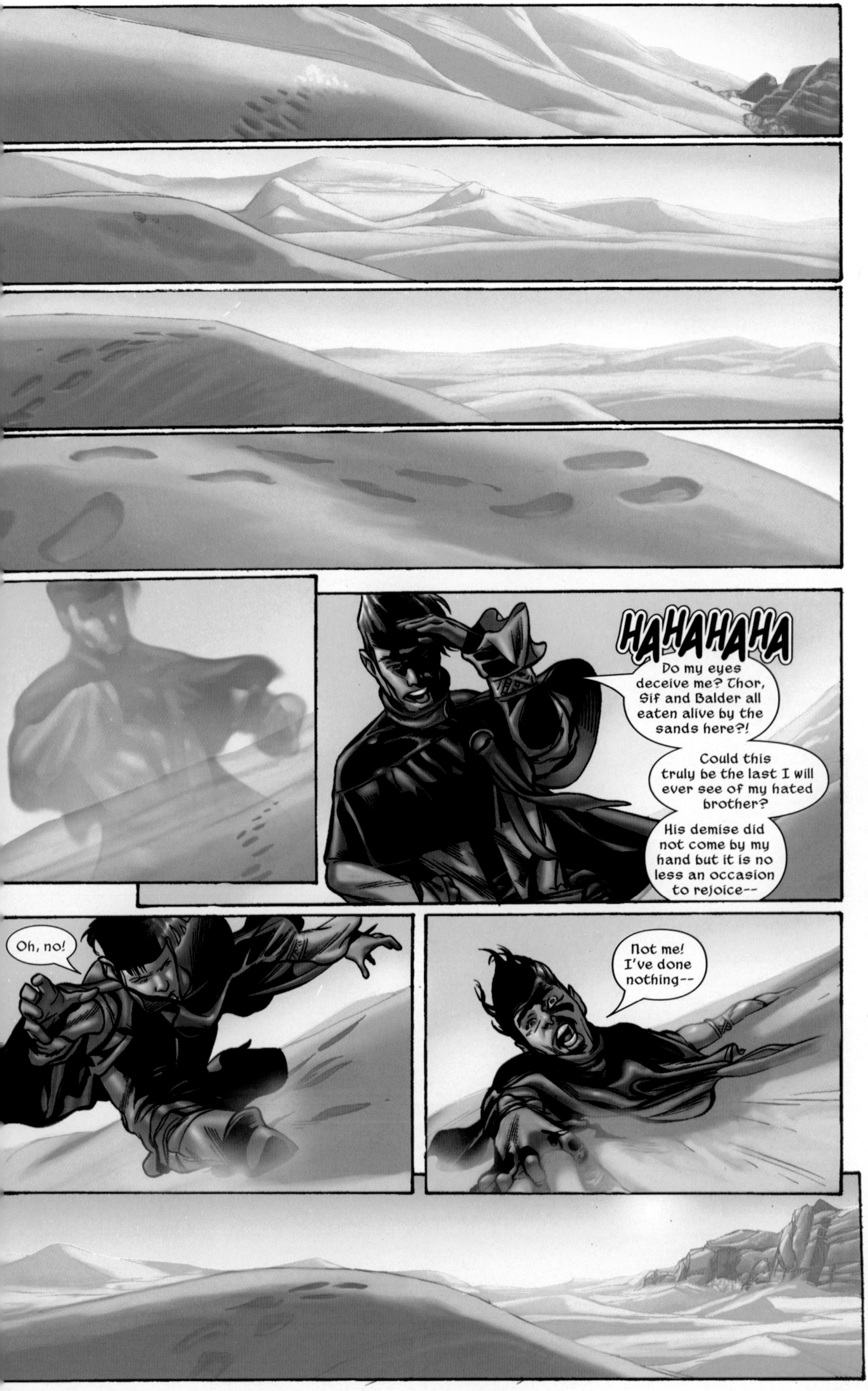
HAHAHAHA
Do my eyes deceive me? Thor, Sif and Balder all eaten alive by the sands here?!
Could this truly be the last I will ever see of my hated brother?
His demise did not come by my hand but it is no less an occasion to rejoice--
Oh, no!
Not me! I've done nothing--

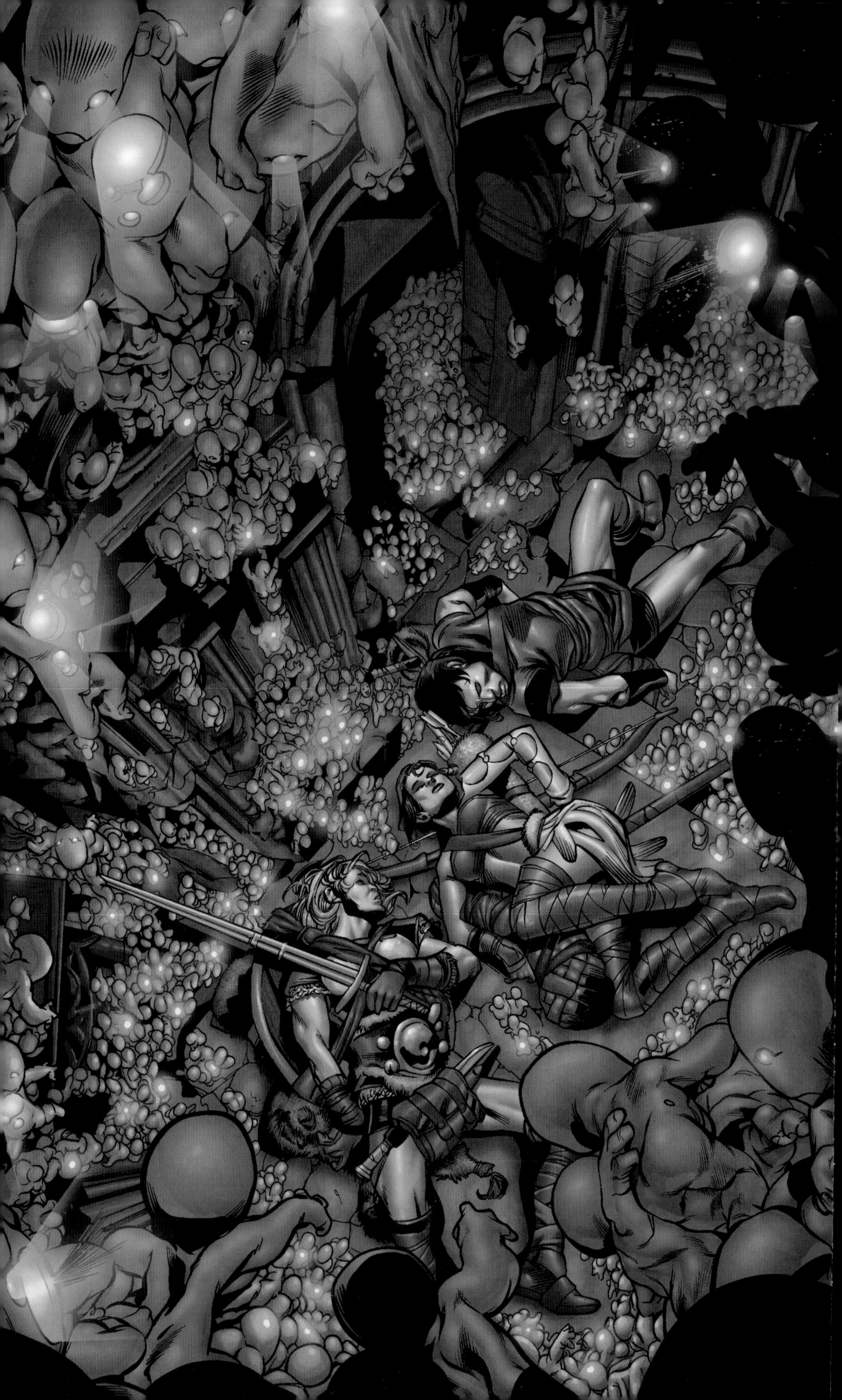

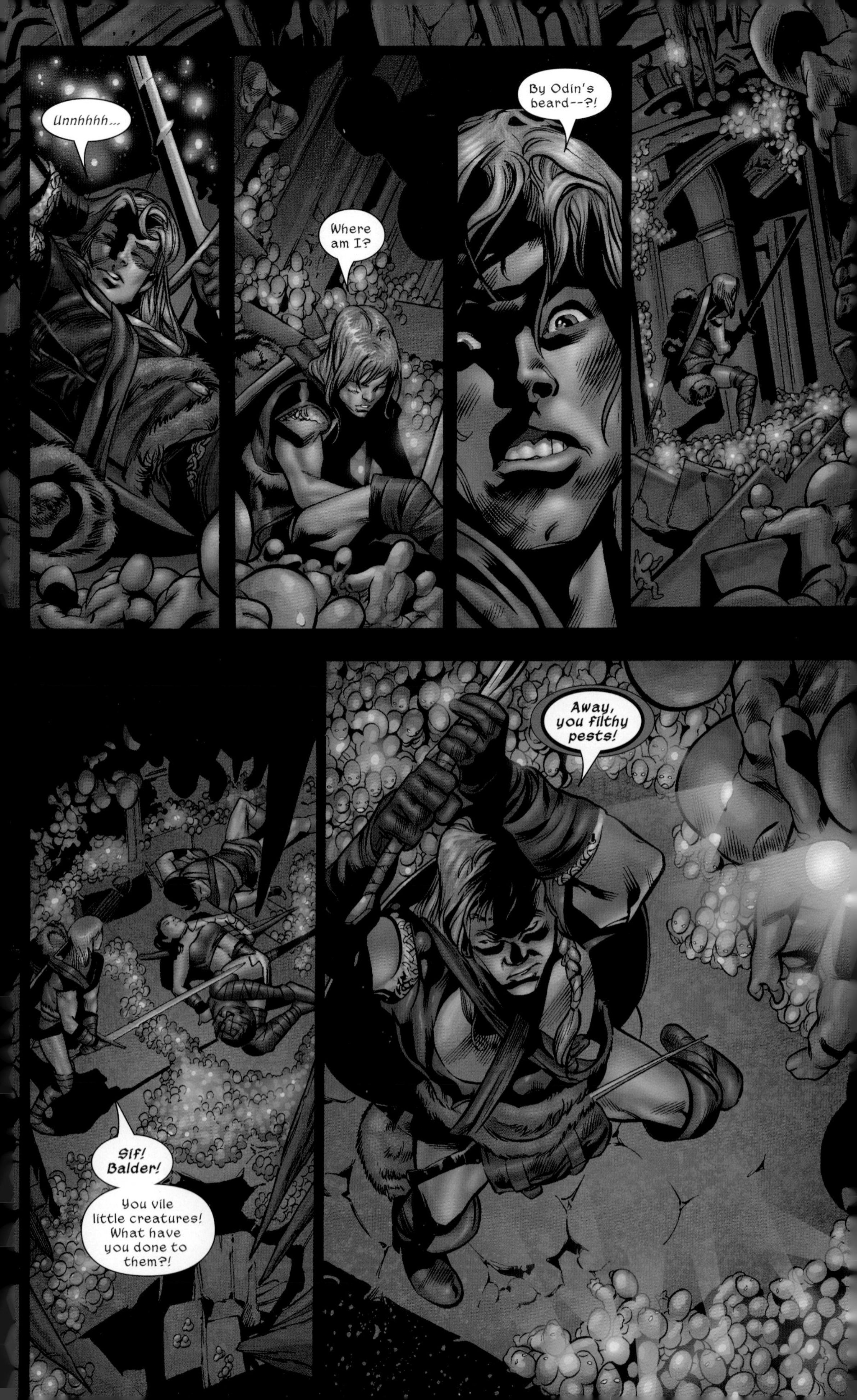
Unnhhhh...
Where am I?
By Odin's beard--?!
Away, you filthy pests!
Sif! Balder!
You vile little creatures! What have you done to them?!

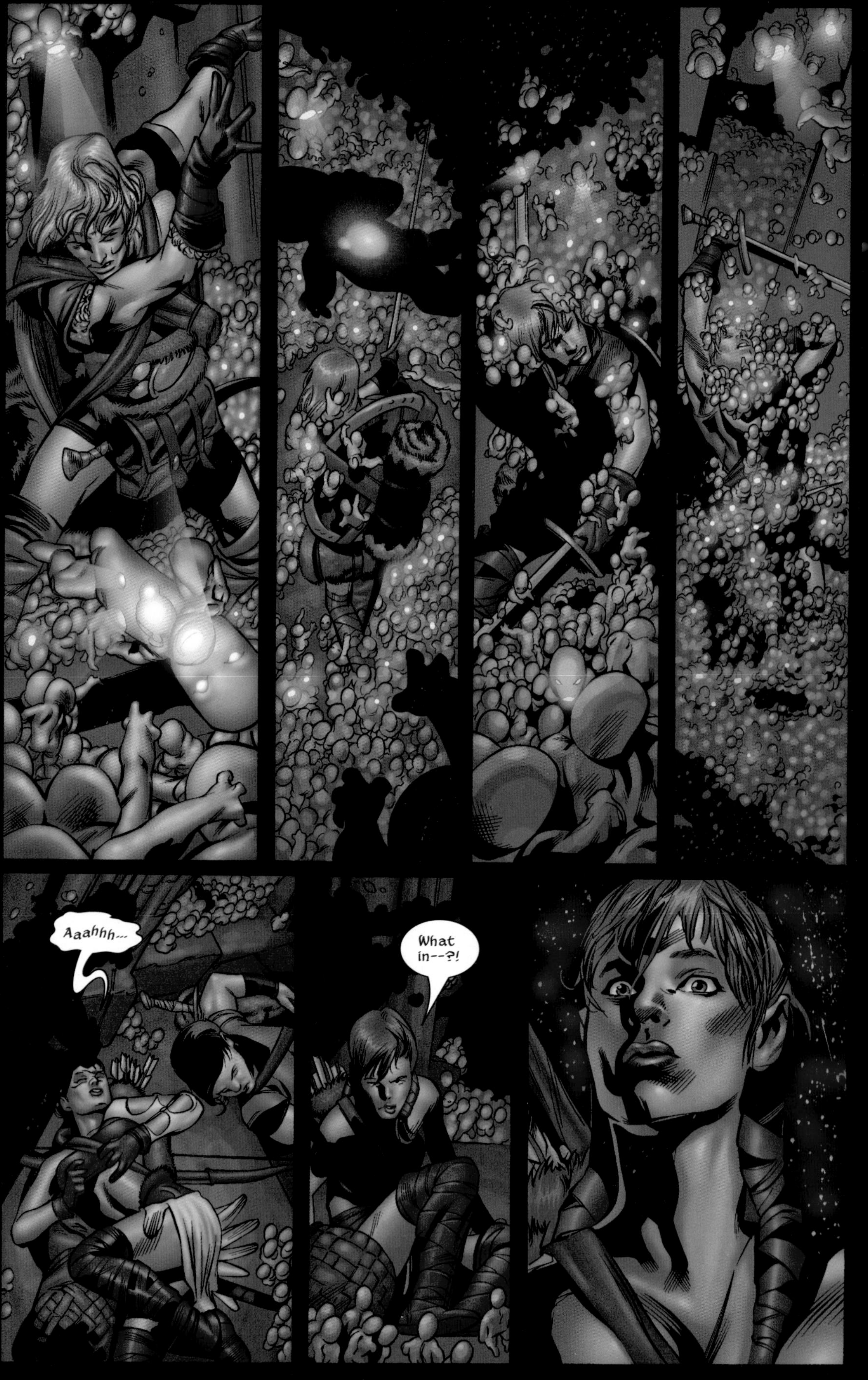
Aaahhh...
What in--?!

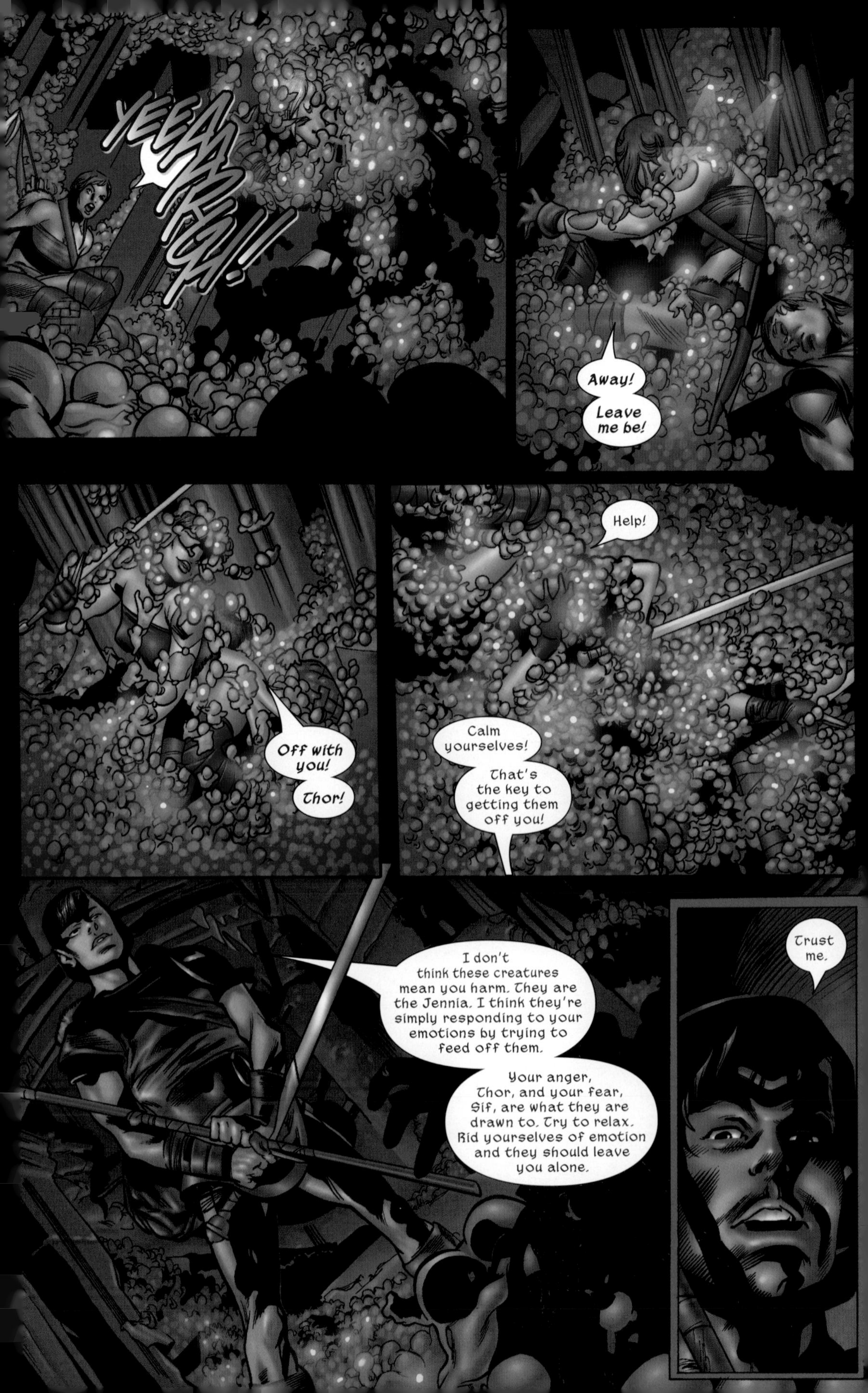
YEEAAARGH!!
Away!
Leave me be!
Off with you!
Thor!
Help!
Calm yourselves!
That's the key to getting them off you!
I don't think these creatures mean you harm. They are the Jennia. I think they're simply responding to your emotions by trying to feed off them.
Your anger, Thor, and your fear, Sif, are what they are drawn to. Try to relax. Rid yourselves of emotion and they should leave you alone.
Trust me.

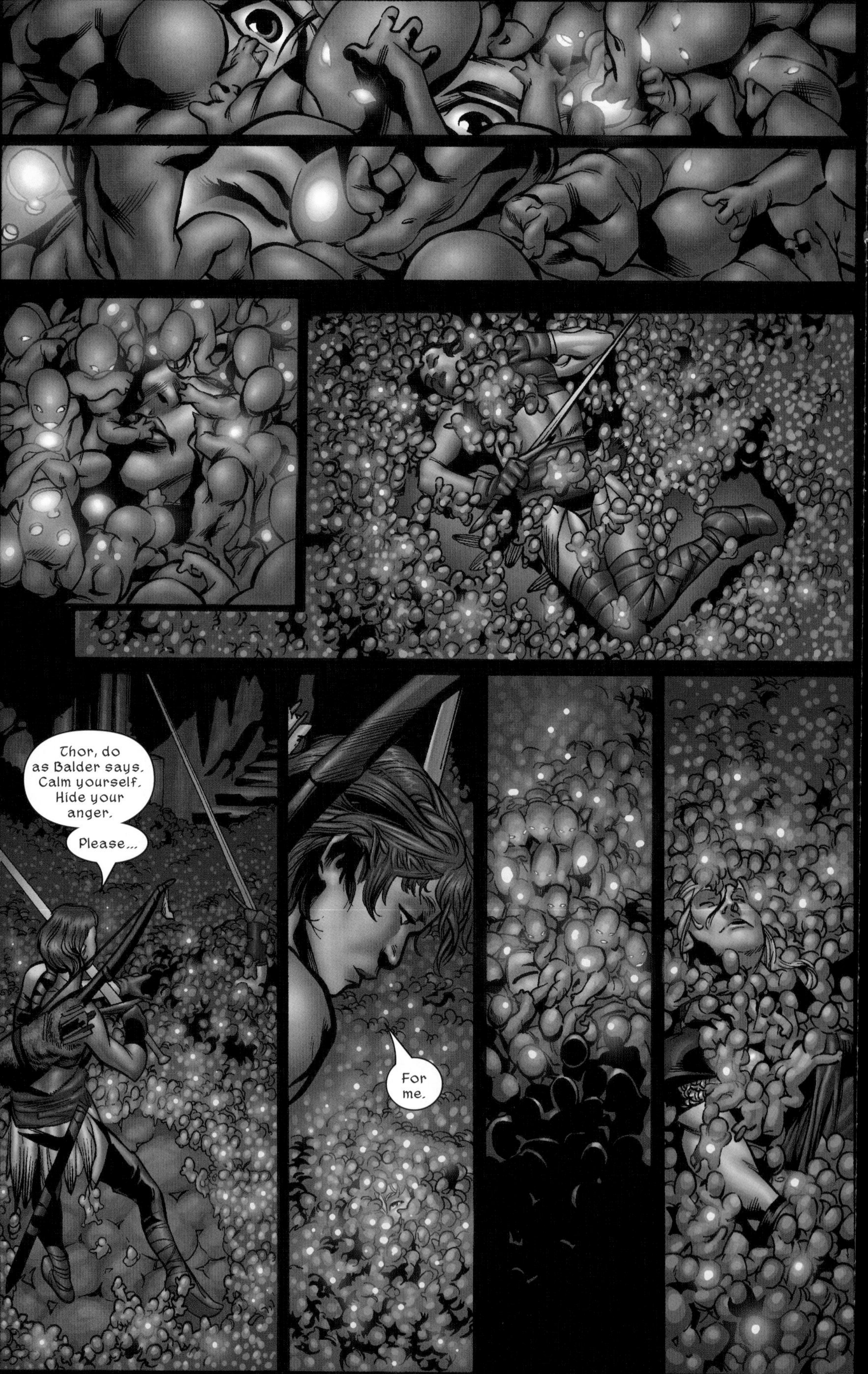

Thor, do as Balder says. Calm yourself. Hide your anger.
Please...
For me.

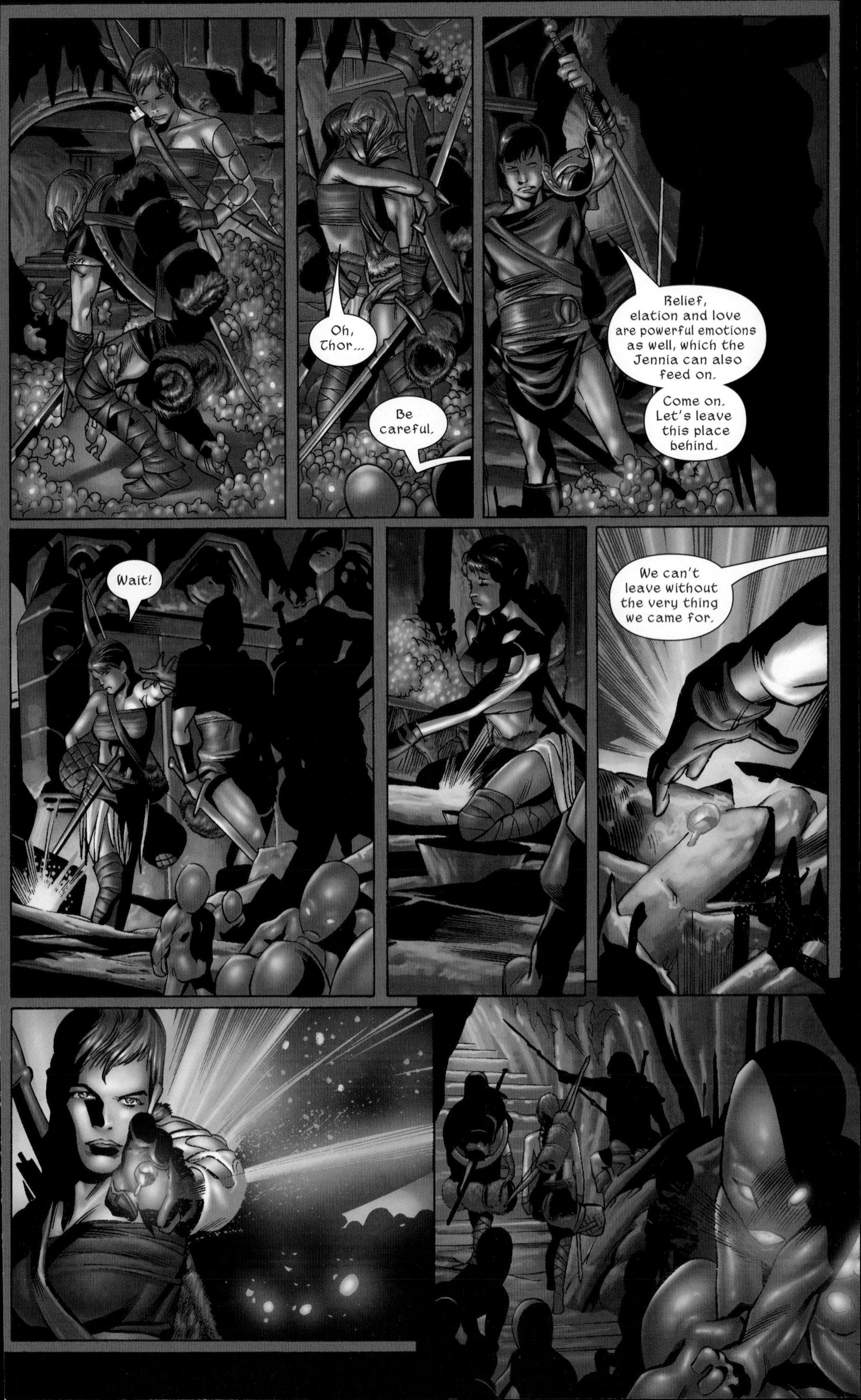
Oh, Thor...
Be careful.
Relief, elation and love are powerful emotions as well, which the Jennia can also feed on.
Come on. Let's leave this place behind.
Wait!
We can't leave without the very thing we came for.

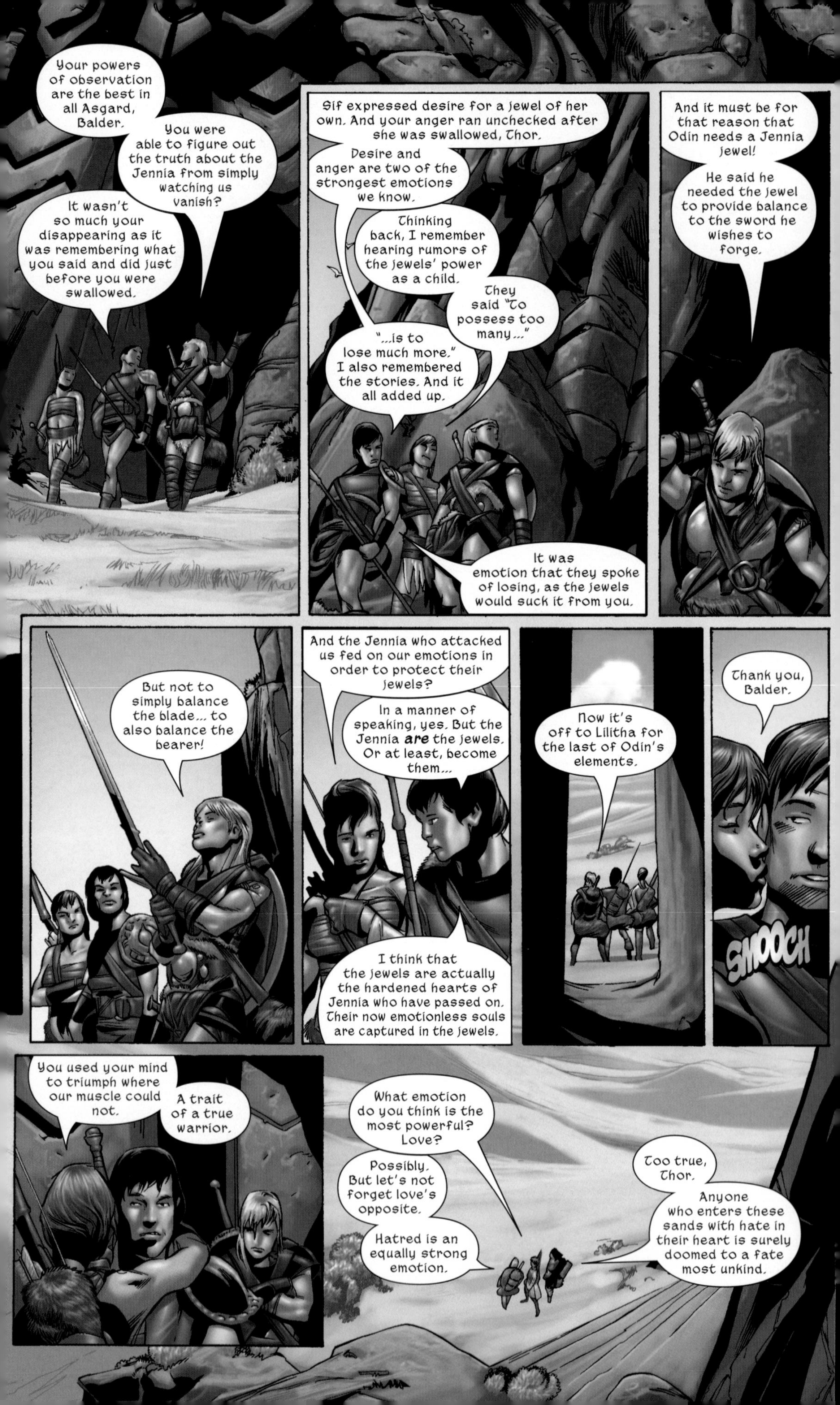

Your powers of observation are the best in all Asgard, Balder.
You were able to figure out the truth about the Jennia from simply watching us vanish?
It wasn't so much your disappearing as it was remembering what you said and did just before you were swallowed.
Sif expressed desire for a jewel of her own. And your anger ran unchecked after she was swallowed, Thor.
Desire and anger are two of the strongest emotions we know.
Thinking back, I remember hearing rumors of the jewels' power as a child.
They said "To possess too many..."
"...is to lose much more." I also remembered the stories. And it all added up.
It was emotion that they spoke of losing, as the jewels would suck it from you.
And it must be for that reason that Odin needs a Jennia jewel!
He said he needed the jewel to provide balance to the sword he wishes to forge.
But not to simply balance the blade... to also balance the bearer!
And the Jennia who attacked us fed on our emotions in order to protect their jewels?
In a manner of speaking, yes. But the Jennia **are** the jewels. Or at least, become them...
I think that the jewels are actually the hardened hearts of Jennia who have passed on. Their now emotionless souls are captured in the jewels.
Now it's off to Lilitha for the last of Odin's elements.
Thank you, Balder.
SMOOCH
You used your mind to triumph where our muscle could not.
A trait of a true warrior.
What emotion do you think is the most powerful? Love?
Possibly. But let's not forget love's opposite.
Hatred is an equally strong emotion.
Too true, Thor.
Anyone who enters these sands with hate in their heart is surely doomed to a fate most unkind.

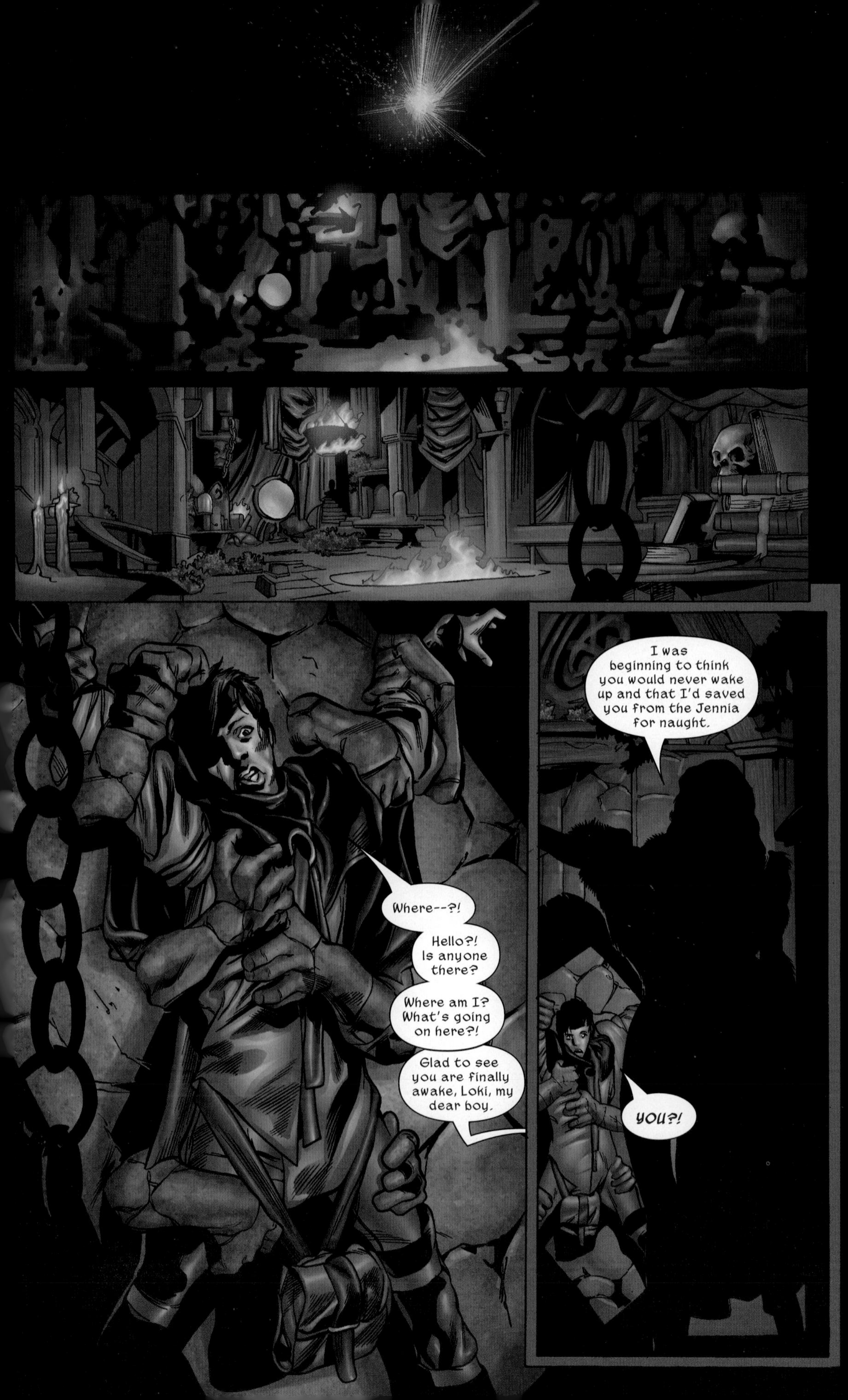
Where--?!
Hello?! Is anyone there?
Where am I? What's going on here?!
Glad to see you are finally awake, Loki, my dear boy.
YOU?!
I was beginning to think you would never wake up and that I'd saved you from the Jennia for naught.

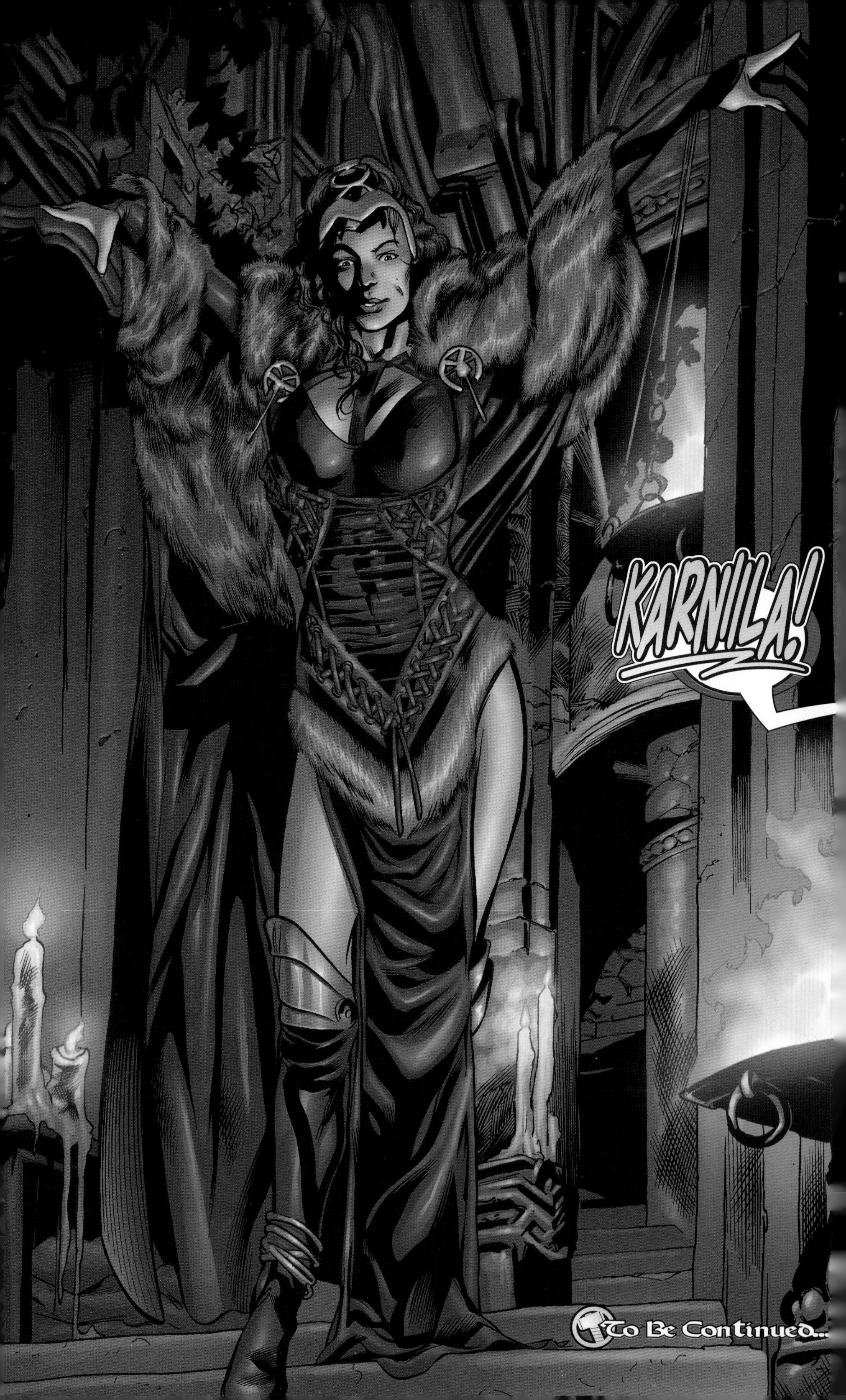
KARNILA!
To Be Continued...